# CHAOS in the *Silence*

Paulami Nath



BlueRose ONE.com
Stories Matter
NewDelhi • London

**BLUEROSE PUBLISHERS**
India | U.K.



BlueRose ONE.com
Stories Matter
NewDelhi • London

For permissions requests or inquiries regarding this publication, please contact:

BLUEROSE PUBLISHERS
www.BlueRoseONE.com
info@bluerosepublishers.com
+91 8882 898 898
+4407342408967

ISBN: 978-93-7310-225-2

Cover design: Yash Singhal
Typesetting: Namrata Saini

First Edition: December 2025

# Preface

The first step towards a great journey started when the little thought crept in…Why?

Why people become silent when they are met with challenges?

Why can't we express what we want to scream out?

The answer for 'why' led me to embark on a solo journey of exploration. Exploration of people's mind, the subtle voices that whispers every time whenever they are juggling through hurdles.

This desperation to speak out, to be able to help people let their feelings out guided me to pen down words into feelings. Poetry is not just a work but a bag of emotions.

It may not give the reader a complete solution but will somehow ease the pain.

With this hope, I lovingly present my first venture of reaching people through pages and bookshelves.

A much needed break from the silence, and an endearing endeavour towards chaos- the silence before storm.

# Acknowledgments

Foremostly, I would like to extend my gratitude to Blue Rose Publication for giving me this opportunity of expressing myself and agreeing to act as a bridge between me and my readers.

I would thank the Almighty for protecting me from all the unseen dangers and blessing me with such parents who have always stood as pillars whenever I needed their support. Their unwavering support made me believe in myself even at times when I did not want to.

And a big thanks definitely goes to the man who silently stood beside me and nodded whenever I needed his validation while sharing his life with me, my dear husband.

Well, last but definitely not the least about whom I have a lot to say.

My little and most critical critic without whom this journey would have never been possible as she never failed to point out the little loopholes which at times failed to grab my attention. Although, I often used to portray her advice aren't even required. But yes, you know you have always tried your best so that my passion remains flawless. Well, I don't want to thank but fine, my little baby sister.

# Contents


| | |
|---|---|
| Life | 1 |
| Bruises | 2 |
| The White | 3 |
| A Fine Day! | 4 |
| The Uncertainty | 5 |
| The Unknown | 6 |
| Wondering | 7 |
| The Untold | 8 |
| It's You! | 9 |
| Words | 10 |
| Turmoil | 11 |
| Need | 12 |
| Wish | 13 |
| Bright Amidst the Odds! | 14 |
| Deep Down | 15 |
| Me | 16 |
| Memories | 17 |
| The Unconscious | 18 |
| Thoughts | 19 |
| Loving in Newer Ways | 20 |
| The Toughest Fight | 21 |
| Lost Days | 22 |

| | |
|---|---|
| Untold Friendship | 23 |
| Sweeter Ache | 24 |
| Loss of a Friend! | 25 |
| Repeat | 26 |
| Power | 27 |
| The Past | 28 |
| Echoes | 29 |
| The Forgotten | 30 |
| An Ear | 31 |
| When I Hurt You | 32 |
| Happiness, An Illusion | 33 |
| My World | 34 |
| Am I? | 35 |
| The Unsaid | 36 |
| Fading Away! | 37 |
| Sitting by the River | 38 |
| When their Eyes Meet | 39 |
| The Full Moonlight | 40 |
| For the Last Time | 41 |
| My Heart! | 42 |
| That One Moment | 43 |
| The Eternal | 44 |
| The Sync | 45 |
| The Re-Discovered Angel | 46 |
| Quest | 47 |
| The Wondering Eyes | 48 |

| | |
|---|---|
| The Garden with High Walls | 49 |
| Completeness | 50 |
| Absence | 51 |
| Destiny | 52 |
| I Met You by Chance | 53 |
| The Wounded Soul | 54 |
| Tune of Life | 55 |
| Someday... | 56 |
| We Feel | 57 |
| Never Thought So... | 58 |
| Souls | 59 |
| Don't Look Deep into My Eyes | 60 |
| You Love Me | 61 |
| Hope | 62 |
| From Roars into Silence | 63 |
| The Last Wine | 64 |
| Waiting | 65 |
| Being Loved Silently | 66 |
| The Melancholy Darkness | 67 |
| Missing You | 68 |
| The Sweet Lady | 69 |
| My Wasted Fancies | 70 |
| Adoring | 71 |
| The Unrequited | 72 |
| Unheard Voice | 73 |
| Still for You | 74 |

| | |
|---|---|
| Black Society! | 75 |
| Wet Feelings | 76 |
| Love with Silence | 77 |
| My Lost Love | 78 |
| Dreams | 79 |
| The Wet! | 80 |
| Dreams of the Rational | 81 |
| Forever | 82 |
| It's Gone! | 83 |
| The Silver Lining | 84 |
| Feelings | 85 |
| You Knew It | 86 |
| Up in the Dark | 87 |
| Fate | 88 |
| That Night | 89 |
| May Be! | 90 |
| Love Persists | 91 |
| Dream to Cherish | 92 |
| The Darkest Eye | 93 |
| A Soft Urge | 94 |
| I Loved You | 95 |
| A Shade of Art | 96 |
| The Fight | 97 |
| The Day You Came | 98 |
| Us | 99 |
| Embracing Us | 100 |

| | |
|---|---|
| The Dark Ally | 101 |
| A Free Bird | 102 |
| Happiness | 103 |
| Cherishing | 104 |
| The Pain | 105 |
| Colour of Love | 106 |
| Happy Days | 107 |
| Reminiscing | 108 |
| Sleepless Nights | 109 |
| The Gift of Absence | 110 |

# Life

Life is a poem,
It's just that you need to play the violin.
Life is a story
It's just you need to sing.
Life is a drama,
It's just you have to express.

# Bruises

I went through stones,
It scratched me, bruised me.
I simply responded to my needs,
Today, I am a stronger version of my softness.
Even with thousands of wounds,
Stronger ever than before.

# The White

We thought of using white bed sheet,
To make it colourful with our love!
But that night never came,
As you left,
Leaving the darkness all around.

# A Fine Day!

A fine day,
I realised that I have given all my feelings away!
A fine day,
You became my oxygen.
A fine day,
I dreamt for the many dreams to come true.
A fine day,
I woke up with my pillow cover all wet!

# The Uncertainty

It's the uncertainty of life,
The uncertainty that rules you.
The un-destined that is waiting
For the unknown to accomplish!

# The Unknown

Drunken me in the thoughts.
In the thoughts of the unknown.
I am clad with the thoughts of my drunken state,
Yet to discover the unsaid,
The unknown!

# Wondering

I stand at the window and wonder
The feeling that I felt.
The charisma of your touch,
Vanishing as fast as it can.

# The Untold

I have loved you since time
You resided in me
As the soul of mine.
Your love, your presence,
A dream of mine.
The tale known to the wet pillows.

# It's You!

It's you and your belief,
It's you and your presence,
It's you and only you,
Marks the difference,
Marks the difference in me.
It's you in whom I am immersed in.

# Words

Words were there to fill in
Ears, you kept aside ignoring me.
Heart, filled with emotions.
You, stood oblivious,
And my heart kept yelling.

Now, that my voice shut,
Your heart wept yelling for me!

# Turmoil

Turmoil in my head,
Chaos in my silence.
Roars in my eyes,
Sinks my soul in itself.

# Need

I felt the need of yours,
And you being mine.
Time passed,
We grew.
The wanting of you pinched me hard,
The smile yet to come.
Dreams drenched in the teardrops,
Ever, forever!

# Wish

The beating of the heart,
Can be heard so dearly.
Eyes wishes to meet.
Fingers long to crisscross,
Lips dried to be kissed.
Souls one!
Wrapped with the warmth of being far enough.
Beauty of love yet being far!

# Bright Amidst the Odds!

It's tough to smile at times,
It's tough to cry at times,
It's rather tough to hope for living at times!
But, still we do smile,
Still, we do cry,
Still, we do hope for our dreams to come true.
It's life!
The most unpredictable,
The most challenging,
The most beautiful.
Bright amidst the odds!

# Deep Down

Deep down my heart,
You reside.
Deep down my heart,
You are buried,
For the last time!

# Me

My mind and soul
Sinking into the ocean.
The ocean of satisfaction.
It asks me to be the sole me.

Wait!
Will I be judged?
For being the sole me?

My mind and soul allows me to be the way I am.
To drink the share of my satisfaction.
The peace of my mind will be mine.
It's forever mine.
I shall nurture it.
And it's my way to be in it!
My mind and soul asks me to be "Me."

# Memories

It's when you are away from me,
It's when you reside in my thoughts,
It's when 'you', I can just feel,
I feel deeper in love with you.
Distance between us,
Memories of ours,
Reminds me of your love to be mine,
Ever, forever!

# The Unconscious

You may think I am foolish
Enough to trust you,
But, you may not imagine,
Your unconscious is revealed!

# Thoughts

The thought laden mind,
The dream laden eyes,
The heart filled with emotions!
What else can be there to drag you?
What else can be there to steal your sleep?

# Loving in Newer Ways

You are the reason for my smile,
You are the reason why I cry!
Believing me in my worsts,
Loving me in my insanity,
You have spoiled me with your love!
Oh my love!
All my insecurities are my fear to lose you,
All my love are here to hold you.
I can't stop loving you even in your worst,
I can't stop loving when you are at your best!
I simply can't get over you,
As I fall in love with you again
And again in newer ways!

# The Toughest Fight

The toughest fight is not with the world,
The toughest fight is not always with a disease.
The toughest fight is with the darkest thoughts of one's mind.
The toughest fight is to shut one's own voice down,
The toughest fight is to control one's own mind!
The darkest of all fights!

# Lost Days

It's those lost days,
Lost days which made me strong.
Waiting for you, made me patient.
My numb heart,
Wet eyes,
Hazy vision through my glass,
Gifted me the stronger me!

# Untold Friendship

He: You are strong. I can never bring tears in your eyes.

She: Stared at him silently gulping the lump in her throat. As he is the one who made her shed tears many a times.

Tale of an untold friendship.

# Sweeter Ache

The motion of your fingers,
The goosebumps on my skin!
With every silver lining on the sky,
My love goes deeper!

With every silver lining of the sky,
My wait goes deeper for you.
With every silver lining of the sky,
I look forward to see you by me.
The wait,
Giving me a sweeter ache,
Resonates your name deeper,
Deeper and deeper!

# Loss of a Friend!

At times it feels,
Friendship can never be lost!
But with the growing time,
The childhood buddies end up
Saying a formal ‘hello’.
The childhood memories get buried
Deep down into the heart,
The memories you wish to cherish again,
Remains a ‘memory’ in the diary of your heart!

# Repeat

Repeat!
Repeat the love,
Repeat the known,
Repeat the done!
Repeat till it reminds the forgotten love!
Repeat, but repeat not the dark,
Repeat not the scar!
Repeat till it resonates the love in the air,
Repeat!

# Power

You have the power to destroy me,
You have the power to mend it too!
You have the power to make me cry,
You have the power to let me be in the pool of sorrow!
You have the ''me'',
That "I" too sometimes is unaware of!

# The Past

The past crumbles you,
Breaking you into pieces.
The past seems to hover over your present.
Making it dull!

But the past is a past happening!
And then you see that face looking at you.
The eyes with love clearing the dust of the past!
Making him glow reflecting on your shadow!

## Echoes

Your voice echoes in my ear,
My heart beats fast with every feeling of yours,
Your touch numbs me,
Your lips utter the unsaid!

# The Forgotten

You are there for everyone!
You try to soothe everyone around you!
You introspect and you feel what others feel.
But, often you are left alone,
You are left hurt!
You are pinched, you are beaten by harsh words.
And, you end up covering your face with a smile.
As your tears aren't seen even by your near ones!

# An Ear

An ear I want!
An ear not judging me.
Several things I have in my heart...
My mind fragile, breaks apart!
An ear I want
An ear listening me,
My mind speaking the unsaid,
An ear not judging me!
My mind stronger enough to fight the scars!
An ear I want!

# When I Hurt You

When I hurt you,
I hurt myself!
When you don't like my few words,
I feel pained for myself!
When you say in a lowering voice,
You don't like certain things,
I then wish to do all the possible things on earth!
I am nothing without you,
I am everything with you!
Your silence tears me apart,
Your smile makes my gloomy day shinier!
I am sorry if I have hurt you ever,
Because, this sorry is to my soul.
As, when you cry,
My soul tears apart!

# Happiness, An Illusion

Happiness, an illusion!
You think it's coming towards you,
But the moment you try to grab it,
It pushes you miles away,
And you are faced with the reality!
Happiness, an illusion!

# My World

You have been my pain,
You have been my fun.
You have been my world,
But why it is such that I feel
I lost my world?
Why it is such that I can't feel the pain anymore?
Is it so, that I am used to the Loss of my World?

# Am I?

I feel peace in my pain,
I feel complete in my pain!
My world has given me immense pain,
Is it so, that I am used to it?

# The Unsaid

The Unsaid remained the unsaid!
The silence spoke for itself.
Eyes searched for the answer,
Ears craved for the unsaid,
Both silent,
Life moved on!

# Fading Away!

A day will come,
I shall fade away.
A day will come,
My 'bindi' would remind you of me!
A day will come,
My voice would echo.
A day will come,
You would pass by my grave
Seeing my man crying at my grave!

# Sitting by the River

Sitting by the river,
The sun is about to set.
The last sunrays hitting straight her face,
They could feel the silence and presence of each other's.
Fingers about to touch,
Hearts beat faster,
Heads felt lighter.
Love was in the air,
A slight resistance stopped them from being each other's.
Silence spoke the rest
As they were bound to be apart!

# When their Eyes Meet

When their eyes meet,
They lose themselves.
When their eyes meet,
They seem to immerse deep into each other.
When their eyes meet,
They again fall in love with each other.
And the world for them becomes musical!

# The Full Moonlight

The full moonlight peeping through the window,
Her face lit up with the dazzling light
making it brighter even more!
The "dark kohled" eyes spoke about the unspoken.
The open hair caressed with finger four.
Her soft pink lips ready to be wet
As wet as my feelings!
My heart beats with breeze touching her hair
And with that I feel losing myself completely into her
As the river merging into the ocean
forever losing its identity.
Her warmth wrapped me enabling to lose myself.
But the heaviness of trust pulled me back.
And I embraced her in the thoughts of mine!

# For the Last Time

You know I couldn't be yours,
You knew my smile wouldn't be yours,
You knew our path would part away!
So for the last time, you looked deep into my eyes,
For the last time you shared me 'Your mine!'

# My Heart!

My heart still pounds as ever before,
My heart still pounds even after knowing you aren't mine.
My heart still pounds feeling the breath of yours,
My heart still pounds hearing your silence,
My heart still pounds knowing the fact we 'loved' each other!

# That One Moment

When that one moment hits me hard,
That why aren't you there for me!
When that one moment hits me hard,
That why ain't I in your arms!
And then that one moment I realise
Had all those I wanted been fulfilled,
It would never have been so beautiful.
Have I had you in real,
The world would have been surreal!

# The Eternal

Her eyes glistens thinking of him
Her heart pounds recalling about him
The slight smile on her face with extreme pain
Breaks his heart apart!
She knew she can't be his
He knew she can't be his
He knew he can't make up to her
She knew they love each other
She knew he isn't hers.
Time had flown.
They kept shut
They have to part away
As they can be only together in a
Platonic way!

# The Sync

The souls beat for each other
The world stops around them
when the eyes meet.
The souls beat for each other
The silence speaks all when the eyes meet.
The souls beat in sync
When their lips touch each other's!

# The Re-Discovered Angel

Amidst the slow breeze,
Music in the air,
Spreading her arms,
She dreamt her dreams...
Her golden brown hair
The little curls of hers,
Twisted like the twist of life.
She dreamt of her future.
She failed in her past,
She lost... and now...
She gained strength,
She stood up
She re-discovered herself.
She is the happy angel.

# Quest

Sometimes we feel sad,
Sometimes we feel bad,
What is there to feel that?
Because love is there to fill the empty in that!

Happiness is not to be find outside,
It is something which is to feel from inside,
People are tired of running and running,
But can someone believe that it is making us cunning?

How is the feeling of love?
It's like flying like a bird called dove...
How great it feels like heaven!
The life in it is eternal.
What are you up to my love?
O my love, its great being with you,
But can you imagine how sad I am without you?
O my love, come to me as as soon,
Else, my life will be at doom!

# The Wondering Eyes

Looking through the windows of the classroom
The wondering eyes,
Wondered the scenic beauty...
The wondering eyes have the upcoming dreams,
It showed everything that they see,
The innocent yet glittering eyes wondered,
Wondered the going-ons of the environment,
The wondering eyes learnt whatever taught,
It imitated exactly what has been given to them!
Ignorant of the materialistics of outer world,
The wondering eyes did not know about
What is waiting for them when they grow up.
The wondering eyes are happy amidst their own world.
The wondering eyes showered immense love silently
Yet resolutely!

# The Garden with High Walls

The garden with high walls,
She never allowed anyone to peep inside her.
Yes, her heart is the garden with high walls.
It was tough to enter...
Feelings were like those precious flowers in the garden,
She closed it from all sides,
She nurtured it,
Then came 'him',
as a ray of light
allowing the flowers to bloom more,
and there were all greenery and bloomings.
He opened the long closed door,
Touched the soul,
It multiplied and glistened.
She is the happy soul.
The door she closed for long
is opened to her soulmate!
She loved it, she rejoiced it,
The happy 'she'
With high walls, difficult to enter...

# Completeness

It's long that she waited,
It's long that she cried alone,
And now it's over...
It's over for her wait
It's over for his mourn.
She loved endlessly.
He cared effortlessly.
He smiled,
She hugged.
And...
The little angel giggled.

# Absence

When I was all alone
In the midst of the ocean of pain
Needed you for sole.
Where were you?
You never looked back
and gave me a hug.
I waited for your coming back.
My eyes kept staring at the long open door.
Only came in is a ray of light.
The thought of your absence shatters me.
Every time I think you are present
Reminds me of your absence.
With the little hope of your presence.
I tried to live my life!
But, it's long that you haven't been present,
Neither you looked forward for me.
I thought about the reason,
But every time there was a question!
What has happened to you
that took me away from you?

I still hope for your presence.
But can just see around your absence!

# Destiny

She sat in the corner of a room,
She missed him
She missed him a lot for years.
Yes,
She wished they could be together
She wished to be his everything.
He entered the room.
Her eyes stuck at his...
They conversed,
A hidden smile at their hearts,
But,
But they seemed to be strangers
Their hearts ached,
Smiling lips still persisted,
Their ways again parted.
She cried,
She cried and confessed
It ached, it hurt...
She waited, waited and waited...
He mourned
(a long sigh)
She became calm
and...
It carried on!

# I Met You by Chance

I met you by chance,
You touched my soul.
The spark in you is unforgettable
Your eyes deep that talks
Your smile elegant, that attracts,
Your presence sparks everything.
The gait in you is phenomenal
The elegance in your tone
mesmerizes the most,
Never knew it would affect so much!
You are the kind of 'sole you'.
You are the 'feel', I wish to feel.
You are the untouched one
I wish to touch.
You are the 'you' I wish to love...
I, met you by chance!

# The Wounded Soul

When I found you, I thought may be
You will too be the same like others,
But you turned out to be the different one.
You touched the wounded soul!
You touched the wounded heart,
You healed it,
You cared for it unknowingly.
You did not know you have affected
The wounded soul so much!
But...
Yes, you did it!
The wounded soul stopped at you.
It tried to live grabbing you,
But then again, you left it all alone.
You left it thinking as a burden
The wounded soul wandering now
Again in the midst of the thoughts...
You, touched the wounded soul!

# Tune of Life

The first look of hers,
The first smile of hers
The touch so tender
Her eyes wander
For the first meet
For the first hug
And the heart beating in sync
Is the tuning for life.

# Someday...

Someday it will stop,
Someday there will be only memories,
Someday it will be all about the missed love...
It is all now, just to resist all the unsaid,
Someday, I will just look into the ray of the light-
For you to come and peep.
Someday, I will not be there,
But my words will pinch your heart,
You will like to care me,
And I will be the invisible one,
And will still love you in the
Platonic way!

# We Feel

Often we feel we are in love,
Often we feel we are the happiest one.
Often we feel we are the best.
But really is it so?
Is the love we feel, actually love in real?
Is being happy, the happiest thing?
Or, waiting for the happiest moment gives happiness?

# Never Thought So...

Never thought it will be so,
Never thought I will be able to love,
You came in just like the cool breeze,
And has penetrated in me,
Making me feel the most completed one.
You have been for me the greatest gift ever.
Never thought without being close physically
The soul will get so much attached!
I wish you to be by me,
I wish myself to get immersed in you,
I wish to be yours,
Ever, forever!

# Souls

Two souls far apart
Yet one!
Two souls silently loving each other,
Yet apart!
Two souls living for each other
Silently with the Unsaid!

# Don't Look Deep into My Eyes

Don't look deep into my eyes,
I will fall for you.
Don't look deep into my eyes,
I will lose myself for you.
Don't look deep into my eyes,
I will forget the world for you.
Don't look such deep into my eyes,
My heart will beat 'only' for you.
Don't look such deep into my eyes,
As I am bound to part away from you.

# You Love Me

When you say you love me,
I feel happy.
When you say you love me,
I feel loved.
I kept your love as the most precious one.
I treasured the love you have given me.
When you say you love me,
I thought it's mine.
When you say you love me,
I could never realise
It's not only mine.
When you say you loved me,
I realised, it was never 'mine'!

# Hope

Looking through the window outside,
The leaves dancing on the tune of the breeze.
I am pensive thinking about the uncertainties of life.
A cool breeze breaking the barrier of the window,
Hitting me, wrapping me in its cold arm.
A freshened mind,
Smiled from inside
Weaving the dreams of the millennium.
Yet, at times dreading for the worst,
And, shattering all my dreams.
But, again I dreamt of the never ending curves to
pursue long.

# From Roars into Silence

There were roars inside me,
Roars of pain, separation, heart-break,
Turning me into pieces.
Pieces of hate, pieces of weep, pieces of cry.
Roars of tyranny spoiled the inner me.
I sat in the corner of a room,
My window panes pale.
A ray of light on my face,
Glistening the pale face of mine.
It tried to wash away the roars that created the upheaval.
The ray of light overlapping the entire dark.
A sense of bliss touched the roars,
You came in, to bring the pieces together.
The broken pieces tried to join.
A new creation of yours,
Turning roars into silence,
A bliss!

# The Last Wine

He knew he can't be mine
So he shared the last wine.
It was all about to be materialistic
And, he shared the last smile.
Both the eyes locked in each other's.
The smile they shared,
Speaking the untold, unrevealed.

# Waiting

The dark sky,
The silver lining giving me the shiver.
The whispering sound of the rain
Asking me to lose myself.
I am in the thought of yours,
I am in the wait for you!
The darkness wrapped me.
The thundering sound crying,
For you to be with me.
But, I am all alone looking at the candle flame,
Thinking of you.
The touch of your fingers on me,
Gives the tinkling feeling.
The soothing touch letting me lose myself
And I am drowned feeling the smell of yours.
And I am still waiting gazing at the candle flame for
you.

# Being Loved Silently

In the crowd of the twinkling stars,
That beautiful pair of eyes smiles from within.
It tries to make eye contact,
But shy too much to look into me.
The busy bees busy in chattering.
He focussed on me.
Once caught staring,
Smiles without uttering one.
So innocent yet expressive.
That beautiful pair of eyes,
Wants to say much.
But, keeps smiling giving the joy
Of being loved silently!

# The Melancholy Darkness

With the melancholy darkness,
Slowly the teary drops of the sky
Fell onto my dreams.
My dreams took its shape,
I drenched into it,
Immersing into the thoughts of the bygone days.
The stars by now separated by the clouds,
Trying to peep towards its onlookers,
And, with that my dreams saw a new phase.
The melancholy darkness is sweeter.
The darkness peeps into the deep thoughts of mine,
Bringing down the tears that shine.
Slowly the teary drops of the sky
Drenched me into the thoughts of mine.

# Missing You

Yes, I miss you,
Not for being still in love with you.
But for the worthless feeling that you gave me.
I miss you,
As you were not supposed to do so.
I miss you when it pains for being so hurt.
I miss you,
As I loved you the hardest.
I miss you,
As you have given me the pain which cannot be healed!
I miss you,
As I wished we could have been together
Only “IF” you wouldn’t have decided to
Leave “ME”!

# The Sweet Lady

The hazy window glass,
Lush green environment.
It's serene, pleasant.
The teary drops of the sky all around!
Gazing into her eyes, I am lost.
Her hazel eyes attracted me.
Her eyes lowered with shy.
And her pink beautiful lips,
Made me nervous.
She passed by me
With utmost grace.
Her smell so beautiful, mesmerising!
It grabbed me making me lose my consciousness.
She sat near me.
Her eyes into mine,
I am losing myself into her eyes,
She touched me with her soft fingers.
The feathery touch of hers
Divine! So divine.
The slight smile of hers, and,
Ah! She is my Sweet Lady,
My sweet dream lady!

# My Wasted Fancies

Amidst the cloudy nights,
I feel your presence.
Amidst the cool breeze,
You still penetrate in me.
I loved you in my dream.
I dreamt you as mine.
Ah! You couldn't realise,
You flew in the sky of your dream.
Leaving aside the thousand fancies knit by me...
And me...?
Kept counting my fancies,
All wasted, wasted and wasted!

# Adoring

In the meadows, amidst the cool breeze,
Penetrating the body and mind.
I follow your footsteps.
Your pink soft feet,
The jingling of the anklet,
Adoring your beauty with a rosy fragrance!

# The Unrequited

It is just to resist what cannot be undone,
It is to keep things to oneself when can't be shared,
It is to celebrate amidst the odds,
It is to love more and celebrate the unrequited!

# Unheard Voice

She screamed aloud,
For her love couldn't be heard.
She wept,
But tears couldn't be seen.
Her heart ached,
Pain couldn't be realised.
A smile persisted on her lips as she
realised nothing will bother!
She couldn't be heard before.
Then came 'he' and wiped her tears,
She couldn't believe her love would ever be responded.
She is calm and composed now
As sinking into him made her forget the unrequited.
He is the prince of her dream now,
Listening to her soundless voice among the millions.
He is the love of hers,
In whom she is lost forever!

# Still for You

Every time I tried to hold you,
You left.
Every time I tried loving you,
You pushed me away.
Every time I thought it will be fine,
You ruined it.
It's okay that you wished to be yourself.
Yet, the love for you,
Still remains the one for you!

# Black Society!

Music all around,
Roars of modernism,
Trends of short skirts, hip hops, jazz, discs.
Yes, I am modern!
I drink, smoke, booze up in discs,
I am modern.
He narrated!
Sound of her cry, her roar... can't be heard!
Scars on her soul, blood shed from within.
He screamed, she wept!
He thrashed, she resisted!
'Please, let me live my way,' she pleaded.

Her mouth was shut with values.
Draped in the traditional attire,
Bounded for the household chores,
Stopped for letting her dream come true,
Yes, he claimed he is being modern,
where a soul died amidst his modernism!
The Black Society!

# Wet Feelings

Looking through my window,
The music of the raindrop
Takes me to the nostalgia.
The love of the unforgotten
And the touch of the millions.
The petrichor instils the feeling of the
missed love of my young self.
The wetness of the weather makes my
Feelings the wettest ever!

# Love with Silence

I was in love with my silence,
I was in love with the sound of my breath,
You entered my silence
Breaking all the boundaries...
You covered me with your smell!
All I could hear is the sound of your breath...
And, I was overwhelmed sinking into you!

# My Lost Love

The love of yours,
I am yet to forget.
The lost me in your smell
Is yet to face the harsh reality.
You left me, but I am yet to recover
the pain given by you.
At times, I embrace it,
At times it gives me the hardest pain.
Still with the cold draught
I feel your presence,
Forgetting that you are no longer mine.
You are happy with your new found love,
Yet, I am to recover my lost love in you!

# Dreams

If it's all about dreams,
Then it must be chased.
Society will pull back,
But you should win the race.
Dreams, all hovering the mind.
Giving a gush of wind,
Shivers from the sleep
Making you feel weak.
Sudden awake from the sleep
It gives the heart throb.
The chains surrounding you,
The cut by it, bleeds.
Move, remove the chains,
The barriers of the society.
The world will point at you,
But you will win,
Leaving behind the weak mind!

# The Wet!

My feelings are wet!
Lying in a couch with gleaming light,
Lightening my dreams,
Your thoughts poked me.
My eyes hazy,
My mind drunken in your thoughts.
You are in front of me now.
The curves of yours so appealing.
The soft you,
Giving me the hardest feeling.
Your curly lash,
Diamond drops,
Your hazel eyes so deep with thoughts,
Your pink soft lips.
Gives a feathery touch.
My feelings are still wet,
As you are gone without being mine.
My eyes still hazy
Gazing for your presence.

# Dreams of the Rational

Holding your hand tightly amidst the beach,
Walking step by step.
Feeling the cool breeze penetrating me.
Looking deep into your eyes,
I embrace the silence hearing its sound all around.
Your arms cozy wrapping me with its warmth.
And the silence has so many things to speak out.
The cool water kissing the feet
Giving me the heart throb feeling of yours holding me.
Your smile tells me the happiness of being with me.
And the silence is wrapping us,
With all the unsaid to be understood by love,
You and me!

# Forever

It is when you want to tie up,
You break down.
You break down amidst the wall of memories.
The wall of memories surround you by its arms.
Taking you to the world of your own.
You and your cherished days,
A piece of nostalgia.

To be adorned forever
Or be forgotten forever!

# It's Gone!

I observed,
I thought
I cried
I smiled
I missed, then became calm.
Thoughts ran across my mind.
Asking me to stop it.
Memories filmed in front of my eyes.
A slight smile at the corner of my lips,
Still hoping for the better.
But,
It's gone.
It's over.
I smile thinking of you.
I cherish our memories.
My smile faded.
Then,
Tears rolled down
Washing away all the
Memories forever!

# The Silver Lining

The silver lining in the sky,
And the pitter-patter!
A beautiful silky bed.
The open blonde hair
And the pink lips.
She smiled with the wet feelings in herself
With the fragrance all over!

# Feelings

Closing my eyes, I see you
I long for those moments of making love
Closing my eyes I feel you
The warmth I am wrapped in
Is what I feel,
Closing my eyes!

# You Knew It

You knew it so well,
You could never be mine!
You knew it so well,
You are going to part away from me.
You tried to gift me the best of yours,
You tried to read my eyes.
And it tried to hide all the feelings,
I knew it so well,
You are never and could never be mine.
But, deep down we are 'each others',
We 'didn't' know it well!

# Up in the Dark

Up in the dark,
There lies a beauty.
A beauty in her solitary.
Eyes deep kohl,
Soft feet.
Walking through the wilderness
The silence of her breath,
Kisses the wandering soul of mine.
Up in the dark,
There lies a beauty
Touching the soul of mine!

# Fate

It's the hope of being charmed, blessed,
It's the hope of a shoulder to lean on.
But the destiny would have decided something else,
It's the fate that would tear apart.
It's the fate that would make you think,
You don't owe being blessed or charmed.
It's the fate that would run you through stones.
And make you the one you never hoped for.
It's the fate that would make you stronger than
ever before.

# That Night

Everything changed since that night,
Friendship faded as love is revealed.
Hearts ached as love flashed!
Smiles covered tears as hearts cried.
Silence prevailed with the awkward chaos in heart.
Everything changed since that night!

## May Be!

You may stop loving the person
Or you may not even reveal to the person about your love.
May be your love couldn't work any more
May be you parted away!
But you will still love the loving days lovingly!

# Love Persists

Their eyes met!
Looking deep into each other's.
He smiled,
She kept looking into him!
Their eyes part away,
The untold feelings buried into their heart!
Love always can't be expressed,
Yet it persists!

# Dream to Cherish

Wanted a touch of yours
To sooth my inner self.
The touch of your hardness
Is all that I wanted
The smile of yours
Wipes away my worries.
But, it's all that I can only wish for...
Because you are a dream not to be fulfilled.
You are only to be cherished from far away
That I wish to dream of every time.

# The Darkest Eye

The darkest eye I met
The shine in those speaks the untold.
The pink lips,
Soothes the skin.
The curve attracts the million.
The golden brown hair is the lightest.
The feet so light,
With the jingling in it.
The turning of yours with the brown hair
And your dark eyes.
The closer we are...!

# A Soft Urge

I couldn't be understood,
As I always wanted to be.
I wanted to be known
By the specially unknown.
One fine day, amidst the crowd,
A husky voice evokes.
The comfort in the voice
Allowed me to be free enough.
The voice so attractive
Soothes me from within.
One fine day,
I wanted to be 'his',
Amidst the crowd
The unknown became the known.
One fine day,
I want to be 'WE'.

# I Loved You

I loved you,
I loved your soul,
I loved your smile.
I loved 'you'
And it's only you,
I loved your flaws.
And, you, sought after my perfection!

# A Shade of Art

A shade of art!
A shade of art it is!
An art of love,
Love in different shades.
Keep on covering every bits
And you will witness a different shade
In each shade.

# The Fight

The smile on my face the next morning,
Is the symbol of the fight, I fought the last night.
Sinking my face into my wet pillow,
And it knew the secret of my pitied sorrows.

# The Day You Came

The day you came into my life,
My eyes experienced new colours,
With you I started weaving new dreams.
Weaving my dreams,
I forgot all the pains caused to me!
With you I have learnt a newer me!
A newer me much happier than ever!

# Us

When I look at the stars,
I remember you.
When I stare out of my window,
I recall you.
I recall those moments,
When you were to come
To hold my hands.
Looking deep into your eyes,
I would forget all my sorrows.
The touch of yours
Would make me forget all my sorrows.
Looking out of the window
I remember you.
The ''US" to be recalled forever!

# Embracing Us

Sitting beneath the hazy clouds,
Embracing the cold breeze
Holding your hands
Looking deep into each other's eyes
I embrace the love of ours
I embrace the 'us'.
The warmth of your presence
The goosebumps of your touch,
Is the 'all' that I wanted
The "US" being together
Is what, is destined.

# The Dark Ally

In the dark ally,
I kept roaming,
Kept roaming for you.
You the man of mine,
Your voice tickles the inner me.
Your lips so soothing.
Your soul the purest one.
I found the bright you in the darkest of mine.

In the dark ally,
I kept roaming,
Kept roaming to finally find you.
You, the magician of my mood.
You, the one whom I am immersed in,
In the dark ally,
I found you to be mine.

# A Free Bird

I am a free bird,
I am free with the brightest wings,
I am a free soul in the darkest of the dark.
I am a free mind,
Whom you lose if you control.
I am free,
At its best if allowed to fly.
I am me,
Who is free from all the shackles!

# Happiness

I used to be happy in my bygone days,
I used to be chirpy in my days of gay.
The smile glistened my soul,
My soul free
And as happy as ever.
I used to be happy in my bygone days.
My bygone days are the days,
Gone ever forever
Taking all my memories of happiness.

# Cherishing

With the gush of wind on my face
The memory of yours, touched my mind.
With the gush of the wind penetrating me,
I remembered the memory of our first meet.
With the gush of the wind,
I cherished the first kiss of ours.
The memory of you,
The smell of yours,
Your warmth, your touch,
Enthrals me from within.
The 'you', the love of yours,
Has ornamented me as never before.

# The Pain

The pain of not being able to see each other,
The pain of missing each other's touch,
The pain of feeling each other's warmth
Is the hardest ever when you are in love.
Yet, eyes meet,
Hearts melt,
Fingers touched,
Smiles persist.
Love didn't fade away,
Distance brought them closer.

# Colour of Love

You are a different chapter of my life,
You are a different story of my life.
You are that special part whom if I share with the world,
The world might get offended
As to why am I supposed to be blessed with such a beautiful chapter of life!
You can't be shared as you are that secret of my life
Where less seemed beautiful!

# Happy Days

Happy were the days we bonded.
Beautiful was the bond we shared!
Now, it's the memories we live in.
It's the bygone days we wish we could hold.

Happy were the days we were together
Memories now keep us close forever!

# Reminiscing

Sitting by the side of the river
Gazing at the sunset,
With the cold breeze hitting the face.
Wrapping me in its cold arms
The soft violin at the background,
My mind at its deepest thoughts.
Reminiscing the beautiful of the memories,
The golden Sun on its way to doom
Letting my memories bury deep into the heart of mine.

# Sleepless Nights

Endless sleepless nights,
Tears caressing the cheeks,
Grief wrapping the mind,
The scars unseen!
She thought she can't smile ever,
Tears, a part of hers!
A beautiful soul peeped the garden of her mind,
Sleepless nights turned to joyous memories.
The love she craved for,
Wrapped her beautiful soul
Forever!

# The Gift of Absence

I will present you
The gift of my absence.
As you couldn't cherish my presence.
All that time I was present with you,
You misunderstood me.
You blamed me and took me for granted.
I cried, I howled, I tried to tell you
how precious you are.
You didn't believe and failed me terribly!
You named it as 'infatuation'
You couldn't return my love.
Now that I am gone
And, you are gifted my 'absence'.
You will miss me in everything
But I won't be there to cherish it,
You will miss the 'ME" till the last of yours
I am the only 'I' whom you can't find everywhere.
And 'you' are gifted with my 'Absence'.